MISTRESS OF SKY AND STARS

Forgotten Gods

LAURA GREENWOOD

Visit Laura Greenwood's website at:

www.authorlauragreenwood.co.uk

Cover by Ravenborn Designs

Mistress Of Sky And Stars is a work of fiction. Names, characters, places, and incidents are the products of the author's imagination or are used fictitiously. Any resemblance to actual persons, living or dead, businesses, companies, events, or locales is entirely coincidental.

If you find an error, you can report it via my website. Please note that my books are written in British English: https://www.authorlauragreenwood.co.uk/p/report-error.html

To keep up to date with new releases, sales, and other updates, you can join my mailing list via my website or The Paranormal Council Reader Group on Facebook.

Blurb

The god of the earth and the goddess of the sky can't stay away from one another...even when they're forbidden to be together.

Nut knows she shouldn't spend all of her time with Geb, but she can't help herself when she's around him.

When their forbidden relationship is discovered, the other gods take steps that Nut never thought possible and bans her from giving birth to the children she's carrying.

Can she find enough allies to reverse the decision and have her babies before it's too late?

-

Mistress of Sky and Stars is an origin story to

the Forgotten Gods series and is based on Egyptian mythology. It includes a dash of adventure, a m/f romance, and can be read as a standalone.

If you enjoy Egyptian mythology, gods and goddesses, quests and adventures, and a modern setting, then you should start the Forgotten Gods series!

A Note On The Gods & Goddesses Of The Forgotten Gods Universe

Due to the span of Ancient Egyptian history, many gods and goddesses took on multiple roles over the span of time. In most cases, the gods and goddesses in the fictional Forgotten Gods Universe have been given one of their various aspects. The family links the Ancient Egyptians formed between their gods weren't meant to represent blood family, but aspect ties. This is why many of the gods and goddesses are consorts with their siblings. In the context of the Forgotten Gods Universe, none of the gods are related to one another by blood, but many choose to create family bonds.

You can see a full list of Gods & Goddesses in the Forgotten Gods Universe, as well as other definitions and information, on my website.

Chapter 1

The feast was in full swing, and as normal, no one was bothering to talk to me. Sometimes I wondered why I was ever given an invitation at all.

Actually, that wasn't true. They invited me because there were so few gods in existence. They couldn't leave me out of it. Perhaps in time as more of us came into being, they'd leave me to do my own thing, instead of insisting I sat down at a feast. It would be better if Tefnut deigned to talk to me, but the other goddess didn't like to, even if she was the one who had created me. In human terms, that made her my mother, but that wasn't really the way things worked. Like all of the other gods, I came from the power surrounding the world. While I could call some of them my family if I wanted to, there was no shared blood between us. Family was something that we chose to be to one another, and Tefnut had decided against any kind of bond with me.

Scanning the room for anyone who wasn't busy proved futile. Ra was sitting on his throne lording it over the rest of us, while Atum stayed aloof on his. For some reason, they considered themselves above us because they'd been some of the first gods to come into existence, even though the rest of us had followed quickly enough and arguably had jobs that were just as important as theirs.

It was a shame Khonsu wasn't here. He was always a lot of fun, but he was busy dealing with his duties as the god of the moon. Before long, I'd need to leave to deal with my own too.

My gaze latched onto a recess behind Thoth's head, and a shadowed figure waved at me.

I didn't even need to see them properly to know who it was. My heart skipped a beat.

Geb. Created at the same time as me, and the one person who seemed to actually *see* me. He wasn't family, but for a whole different reason to why Tefnut wasn't.

I checked that no one was paying me any attention even though I already knew they weren't, and got up. It was tempting to hurry, but I knew that would draw unwanted attention, so made sure to walk past the feasting gods at a leisurely pace. None of them questioned where I was going, they didn't care.

Geb had retreated further back into the dimly lit corridor so he couldn't be seen from the main hall. Which was perfect for me.

He reached out and caught my hand in his, pulling me further into the darkness.

"Nut." The reverence when he said my name was hard to ignore.

"We shouldn't be doing this," I whispered hastily as his hand skimmed over the skin of my arm.

A knowing smile spread over Geb's face. "We were made to do this."

I bit my bottom lip, trying not to give in to the temptation in front of me. "Just because we were created to do something, it doesn't mean we have to do it," I pointed out.

He reached for me and tugged me to him.

A tiny part of me wanted to protest, but the rest of me screamed for more of his touch. It was as if something deep within us connected on a level I couldn't begin to comprehend.

No matter how many times I'd tried to stay away from Geb, I always ended up back in his arms.

"I won't force you," he murmured, his breath fanning against the delicate skin of my neck. "If you tell me you don't want to spend time together again, I'll respect that."

There was no missing the hint of doubt in his voice. Not that he thought he wouldn't respect me, but because he knew it was pointless to try to deny the connection between us.

I reached up and cupped his cheek in my hand. "I never thought you would," I promised. "You're too good of a man to even consider it."

A doting smile stretched over his face, and sincere innocence entered his gaze as he looked at me. No matter how many times we were together, it was clear that Geb had no idea how dangerous what we were doing was. We might have been created to be a pair as the sky and the ground, but I doubted the other gods would like the closeness of the bond between us. Peace was fragile enough as it was, we didn't need to make it worse.

I glanced over my shoulder, checking that none of the others had followed us from the feast. Once I was certain they hadn't, I pulled Geb to me with the hem of his tunic and crushed my lips against his.

He wrapped his arms around me, pulling me tighter and deepening our kiss. I melted into him, knowing that the fact the others would frown upon us doing this only served to make us want it more. They'd created two halves of a whole, which made it impossible to fight what was between us.

Not that I really wanted to. Up until the moment we'd given in to our feelings, I'd never really considered this kind of relationship. I doubted if any of the other gods had either. It was something none of us had a need for according to our state of being.

But when I was with Geb, everything

seemed so right. As if the wrongs of the world no longer existed, and everything was about the two of us and how we existed relevant to one another. It put everything else I'd ever wanted into perspective.

We pulled away from one another, and simply stood for a moment, our breathing ragged and our gazes locked. His hazel eyes bored into me, seeing the truth in my soul that no one else had even tried to find.

"You're sparkling," he whispered.

I broke eye contact with him to glance down at my arms. Sure enough, my dark blue skin glittered despite the dim light.

I sighed. "Having starlight embedded in my skin doesn't bode well for managing to sneak around," I quipped.

"I think it's beautiful." He reached out and brushed my cheek with the tips of his fingers. I assumed that must mean the stars were shining there too.

"It might be, but it also makes life more difficult than it has to be."

"Can you turn it off?" he asked.

I frowned. Could I? Now there was a question. From what I could see, the brightness of the stars on my skin varied based on my emotions, and the happiness I felt when I was alone with Geb had brought them out this time. But I'd never tried getting rid of them. Like all of the other gods, I could change aspects of my appearance at will, and sometimes create glamours. I'd made myself the same deep bronze as Tefnut once, but had turned my skin back to its natural dark blue after a matter of hours. It felt more me that way. But I hadn't erased the stars. I didn't want to. They were part of me and my role as a sky goddess.

"I don't think so, but I've never tried," I voiced my thoughts aloud so he could be part of them.

"Never do," he responded, taking me a little by surprise. "They're part of what makes you who you are. I wouldn't want that to change."

A small smile spread over my face as warmth rose inside me. I wanted him to feel that way about me, more than I wanted to be that way about myself.

Raucous laughter sounded from the direction of the feasting hall, pulling me away from the tension between us.

"We should get back." It was hard to keep the disappointment out of my voice. If it was up to me, I'd be able to spend all the time with Geb that I wanted, but we both had duties which couldn't be ignored, and one of those was to spend time with the other gods so that humans knew where we were should they need our help. Personally, I thought we should find a better system. It was counterproductive for all of us to be on call at all moments of the day. We should have help. There was no way we could keep up this amount of work and support for the human race if we didn't have people helping.

But no one would listen to me if I suggested we started some kind of priesthood, they didn't seem to think I was important enough. I couldn't even get Geb to voice the idea for me as they felt the same way about him.

Nothing about this system was going to work for a long time.

"I can come to your chambers tonight if

you want?" he asked, bringing me back to the present.

I nodded. "I would like that."

He pulled me in and pressed another swift kiss against my lips. I melted into him once more, accepting everything he had to give me and still hoping for more.

We had to return to the feast and the other gods, but we could be the two of us for a moment longer first.

Chapter 2

I listened for the tell-tale footsteps outside my door which would announce Geb's arrival. Thankfully, my chambers were large enough that no one would think twice about someone stopping by. And even if they did, they wouldn't immediately jump to the right conclusion. It was only going to be a problem if the others noticed how much time Geb and I were spending together.

Which meant we should stop. Despite knowing that, I couldn't find it within myself to even consider it. I wanted to spend every day with him. It'd be every hour if I could. None of the other gods ever talked about feeling this way.

Every now and again, I found myself wondering if there was something wrong with me, but it didn't seem right that feeling so alive and so cherished could be wrong. They were the ones missing out on something, not me.

The beaded curtain covering the door rattled as Geb stepped through it and into my room. My heart skipped a beat as he strode over to me, his confidence only inspiring more of my need to spend time with him.

"Did anyone see you?" I asked. I might want to be with him, but that didn't mean the other gods would be particularly understanding if they'd seen him coming into my rooms. One visit wasn't going to raise any eyebrows, but visits almost every day were a different story. Which was why it was easier for us to be cautious all the time. There'd be fewer chances of anyone picking up a pattern and working out what was going on.

"I don't think so," he responded. He reached out and pulled me to him, but I put a hand on his chest to stop him from coming any closer. Just for a moment.

"Are you sure?" Sometimes, I didn't think he was as serious about keeping things under wraps as I was. I didn't know why when the fallout would impact him too, but it always seemed to come down to me to keep us safe.

"Nut..."

I sighed. "I'm sorry."

He reached out and brushed a strand of dark hair away from my cheek. "I promise, I understand why this is important."

"I know."

"Do you?" There was only a hint of accusation in his voice and it wasn't entirely unwarranted when I was questioning him.

I closed my eyes and took a deep breath. There was no way he was going to turn this around on me. "I know you understand," I started, even though he was right, and I wasn't completely convinced of that yet. "But sometimes, you don't act like it."

"All right, I'll make more of an effort to make absolutely sure I'm not followed when I come to meet you."

"Thank you," I whispered.

Reassured, at least for the moment, I snaked my arm around his neck and pulled him down so our lips met. I melted into our kiss, relieved that the serious part of the evening was over and we could focus on something which would be much more fun for both of us.

He kissed me hungrily, letting me know that despite my reservations about his sneakiness, he was motivated by the fact he wanted me.

I broke the kiss and took his hand in mine. I pulled him through to my bedchamber and let go so I could pull my dress over my head. He stared at me hungrily.

I laid down on the bed and waited for him to join me, stretching out my body and not feeling the slightest bit of self-consciousness. How could I when he looked at me with hunger in his eyes?

Geb stripped off his kilt and got onto the bed beside me, his hands roaming over my body. A whimper escaped me as his fingers sought my entrance.

He leaned in and caught my lips with his as he pushed inside, making me squirm with anticipation as desire grew within me.

"More," I murmured into the kiss.

He chuckled and used his thumb to press against my most sensitive place. I gasped and arched up into him. He didn't stop, and kept up until my world spun and a release crashed over me.

I let out a satisfied sigh and pushed him down onto his back so I could straddle him. The room filled with light from the stars embedded in my skin as we moved back and forth, the intensity of the connection I had with him making them shine brighter than ever.

Geb's fingers squeezed into the skin of my hip as I moved back and forth, sending us both closer to the edge. I let out a moan as the pleasure almost becomes too much, and I lose the ability to keep up the pace.

With an ease that I could never match, Geb flipped me onto my back and took over. I arched my back and slid my hand down between us so I could touch myself as he moved.

I gasped as I found my release, my body shaking and the starlight intensifying even more as a result. I was dimly aware of him tipping over the edge alongside me, but I was too caught up in the pleasure vibrating through my body to truly notice.

I collapsed back onto the pillow, my breathing shallow and the world seeming a little bit more hazy than it had before.

Geb laid down beside me and opened his arm so I could put my head on his chest. I smoothed my hand over it and let out a satisfied sigh.

"Remind me why we're not supposed to do this again?" I murmured.

He chuckled. "Probably because some of the older gods don't want us creating alliances between ourselves that they don't have control over."

"The more of us there are, the more likely that's going to be."

"They'll come around to that way of thinking eventually," he assured me. "But for now, they're going to continue doing things their way."

"True."

He leaned in and kissed the top of my head. I let out a soft hum.

"So long as we can keep doing this, I don't mind," I said.

"I don't either."

My eyes drifted closed and the threat of sleep overtook me. But that was fine. Right now, I was safe in Geb's arms, and that was exactly where I wanted to be.

Chapter 3

I stretched out on the bed while Geb traced constellation lines between the stars on my back. I closed my eyes and enjoyed the sensation, loving how it felt to have him touch me.

Voices came from down the hall outside, and both of us froze. We exchanged worried glances, then pulled apart, but didn't move away from one another. There was a chance, however slim, that whoever was coming this way didn't want to talk to me, and if that was the case, then we were in the clear.

Somehow, I didn't think we were in luck.

"I'm just going to go and see Nut..." Taweret's voice drifted through the beaded door.

"Get up and dressed," I whispered to Geb, throwing off the blanket and grabbing my dress so I could pull it over my head. I smoothed down the fabric and fixed my hair in the hope that it was at least a little bit presentable.

Geb belted his kilt, already looking more presentable.

Taweret's footsteps were surprisingly loud and I found myself dreading her entrance. I actually liked the protection and fertility goddess, but she was definitely about to catch us together. Whether or not she reported it to the other gods would depend on if she thought it was noteworthy for Geb to be here. I ran through the other times we'd been caught, trying to recall whether or not she'd been there, but it was pointless, I'd always been focusing on other things.

"The senet board," I whispered, pointing to where the board game had been abandoned mid-game a few nights ago when we'd gotten distracted.

Geb nodded and went to sit on one of the reed mats next to the board.

I took a moment to compose myself. I

wouldn't have long enough to check my reflection in the polished gold plate in the other room, which was a pity.

I scanned the room to make sure nothing was out of place. My gaze snagged on a pitcher of water and two goblets, so I scooped them up. It would help make it look like we'd been playing for longer than we had.

With a quick glance over my shoulder to make sure Taweret wasn't about to walk into the room right away, I hurried over to Geb and handed him one of the goblets, before splashing the cool water into it.

The beads rustled as I was finishing. My heart pounded faster than was entirely comfortable, but I plastered a smile on my face all the same.

"Ah, Nut, you aren't alone," Taweret said, though there wasn't even a hint of accusation in her voice. We might be able to get away with this after all.

"No, Geb and I are in the middle of a game of senet, I'd invite you to play, but..." I waved my hand. It was the only game any of us partook in, I didn't need to tell her that it was only for two players.

She waved my apology away. "It's no trouble, I'm not very good at it anyway."

"Ah." I wasn't sure what to do with her admission, or what to say in order to make the whole situation seem less suspicious.

"Tefnut sent me," she said.

I grimaced. What did she want? "Oh, is everything all right?"

Taweret shrugged. "Who knows with her? I think she just didn't want to go through the effort of getting off and coming to find you herself."

I raised an eyebrow. That was almost disapproval in the other goddess' voice. I wasn't about to push her to elaborate though. The last thing I needed was for my dislike of Tefnut to get back to her. She wasn't the kind of woman who would let it slide.

"What does she want?" I asked.

"She wanted you to know that she expects you to wait on her at the next festival."

I sighed. "And she felt the need to send a messenger for that?"

Something like amusement flitted over the other woman's tanned face. "Apparently."

"Thank you for telling me," I said as

politely as I could muster. It wasn't Taweret's fault that Tefnut was using her as a lowly messenger, and I wasn't about to alienate a powerful deity just because one of my creators wanted to be petty. That would make me as bad as her, and if there was one thing I was determined to do, it was to stay classier than Tefnut.

"You're welcome." She paused as if wanting to say something else.

I waited, not wanting to scare her away from whatever it was.

"I may not be a good senet player, but I do love a good hunt. If you want a partner for one, let me know," she offered.

Surprise flooded through me. I hadn't expected an invitation like that one. It meant a lot that the other woman would extend it to me.

"I will, thank you."

"Sooner rather than later, if you don't mind. I think we could become fast friends, Nut," Taweret said.

A genuine smile spread over my face. "Perhaps we could go in a couple of days, I don't believe I have any duties to occupy me then."

"We'll discuss plans tomorrow over breakfast?"

"That sounds good to me," I agreed, finally feeling like I was going to find the one thing I'd been looking for since I came into being.

"Enjoy the rest of your game." The smile and wave she gave me were completely genuine. "You too, Geb."

"Thank you, Taweret," he responded, dipping his head in respect.

None of us said anything as she disappeared back through the beaded curtain, no doubt on the way to her own chambers. If we were going to be friends, then it was best if I found out where they were at some point.

"That went well," Geb said.

"Surprisingly so," I admitted.

"Shall we pick up where we left off?" he asked, raising an eyebrow and looking back towards my bed.

I shook my head. "Do you mind if we sat and played for a little bit?" I gestured to the senet board. I needed a chance to calm down after nearly being caught with him. Even if I didn't think Taweret thought anything of the two of us being in the same room, it was still too close for comfort.

"Of course. Why don't I reset the pieces and you can get some wine?" he asked.

I nodded. That was a good idea. I had a jar stored in one of the baskets to the left. It wasn't the best the temple had to offer, but it would do the job.

"What do you think Tefnut wants?" he asked, as he moved the pieces into the right positions to restart the game.

I shrugged. "To remind me that she can control my life if she wants to."

"And everyone else around," he muttered.

I pulled the jar of wine out of the basket. "That does sound like Tefnut."

"Why is she like that?"

"Who knows? Maybe she thought she was going to be the only goddess and would be special because of it?"

I rejoined him on the mats, and held out the wine to ask if he wanted some. He downed his water in a few gulps so I could fill up his cup. After his was filled, I moved on to my own.

"That's sad."

"It'll change over time." I hoped. There was no way she could keep it up forever, and that was how long we were looking at so long as no one worked out the specific way each of us could be killed.

"Hmmm." Geb clearly wasn't convinced.

"Why don't you start?" I gestured towards the senet board. "I did last time, it's only fair."

He snorted. "You're still going to win."

"Probably," I admitted. He wasn't particularly good at the game. "Maybe it's because I can actually go to the afterlife if I want to."

"Why would you want to?" he asked.

I shrugged. "I imagine there must be some kind of duty for me to do there that I don't know about yet. We'll find out in time."

"Hmm, true. Though I'm not sure your ability to travel to the afterlife has much to do with senet."

"Maybe not. Or maybe it's just because I practise. If you did that more, maybe you'd be better," I teased.

Geb chuckled. "Is that why you keep playing with me?"

"Yes. It's no fun beating someone who plays so badly."

The more time passed since Taweret's visit, the more relaxed I began to feel. This was what I wanted from the time I spent with Geb. Hopefully, one day I'd be able to do it without all of the sneaking around.

If I was lucky.

Chapter 4

I hummed to myself as I drew a comb through my tangled hair and threaded beads into it. The main festival of the year wasn't for another few months, but that didn't stop the rest of the gods from wanting to have small celebrations at other times, and today was one of those. Thankfully, all we'd have to do was sit and feast, then talk to any of the humans who happened to have a problem.

Luckily, while we could hear their problems today, we didn't have to do anything about any of it until tomorrow. Not that I got a lot of requests I could act on anyway. Most of them revolved around things I had no control over. No one seemed to understand that it was Ra who controlled the light from the sun, and Tefnut who made it rain. The only thing I had any control over was the twinkle of the stars in the night sky. At least I did a good job of that.

But it didn't help when people came to me asking for help of some sort. I looked like a fool when I tried to explain, especially when neither Ra nor Tefnut seemed particularly interested in helping me field the questions.

I closed my eyes and took several calming breaths. I couldn't let them get to me. It wasn't worth it. The only person I could control was me.

The rattle of the beads hanging from my door broke my thoughts. I set down the comb and rose to my feet, making my way around the screen which separated my dressing area from the rest of my space.

"Daughter," Shu said as he walked through the door without even asking if I was available.

I was instantly on edge. He didn't claim any kinship with me any more than Tefnut did, and I was fine with that. They let me live my life tending to the sky, and I left them to their work with the air and moisture.

"I'm just about to leave," I said, waving to the door in an unnecessary way. Geb was expecting me, and I didn't want to keep him waiting for too long in case he thought I was standing him up. Especially as we wouldn't be able to get much time together later.

"This will only take a moment." He indicated to a pair of low stools.

I bit my lip and tried not to take offence at the fact he was ordering me about in space which was supposedly my own. Despite that, I took a seat and waited for him to get to the point.

"You're to stay away from Geb," he said sharply.

I raised an eyebrow, trying not to betray the slight panic that was building within me. As far as I knew, we'd been subtle and no one should know about the two of us. Certainly not a god who rarely paid me any attention. "Why?"

"You're not to be too close to one another. If you are then you will cause no small amount of trouble," he said ominously.

"Is that all?" I asked coolly, though the flickering of the stars on my skin might give away my nervousness. How did he know about us? We'd been as careful as possible, and I hadn't even told Taweret about my relationship with him, and she had quickly become my closest friend.

"This is a serious matter," Shu said, his expression underlining the tone of his voice. He truly did think what he was saying was important. Perhaps it was, but I didn't like the implications that everyone thought they could boss me around.

I got to my feet, not wanting to listen to any of this any more.

"This isn't coming from me, Nut," he said quickly.

I froze. That wasn't good. There weren't many people who could order Shu to deliver a message, and all of them were more powerful than I was. I didn't think they'd do anything to put an end to my existence, they needed me too much, but they could make my life miserable.

"Who?" A small part of me didn't want to know so I could continue living in denial, but I knew that wasn't going to get me anywhere. If I had to be careful of someone, then I'd much rather know.

"Hope you never find out," he muttered darkly.

I stared at him for a moment, trying to think of the best response to that which wouldn't make me sound like an idiot. I wasn't convinced there was one.

"I won't take up any more of your time," he said, getting to his feet. He flashed me an uncomfortable smile. At least this was as bad for him as it was for me. "I hope to see you at the feast later. And that you think about what I've said. This is serious, Nut. You won't like the consequences if you don't heed the warning."

I opened my mouth to respond, but he was already disappearing out into the corridor, no doubt back to whatever tasks he had to do which were more important than this one.

It took me a few moments to regain my thoughts. A small part of me wanted to do what Shu had said and stay away from Geb, but that didn't sit right. Especially when he was the only person I wanted to see right now.

He'd know what to do about it, and would assure me that there was nothing to worry about it.

Before I knew what was happening, I was out of my room and on my way to his, looking over my shoulder every time I turned a corner to make sure no one was following me. They weren't. I suspected everyone was getting ready for the festival, and that very few of them actually cared what I was doing with my life.

I slipped into his chambers, relieved to find him alone and waiting for me. I raced to him, wrapping my arms around his waist and squeezing him tight. He returned my embrace, rocking the two of us back and forth, but not saying anything. He must have sensed that I needed comfort more than anything else right now.

"What happened?" he asked once I'd pulled away.

I let out a loud sigh. "Shu warned me to stay away from you. He said the instruction had come from someone else."

"Who?"

I turned to where I knew he kept dried

fruit and wine, pulling some out for the two of us to break our fast with. We wouldn't want to eat too much before the feast, but it was never sensible to go without eating for too long.

"I don't know," I admitted. "I presume it has to have come from above him."

"Which leaves Ra, Atum, and Amun."

"I doubt it was Amun." He was the kind of god who kept to himself and truly didn't care what the rest of us were up to.

"Agreed." Geb nodded. "And Atum thinks we're all too beneath him."

"Which leaves Ra." Who had been the most likely candidate in my eyes anyway? The sun god was prone to these kinds of dramatics, particularly when he thought someone could become more important than he was. What didn't make much sense was that there was no way I was ever going to be that. He was the reason the world had been able to flourish. Without the sun, there would be nothing. All I did was provide something for that sun to travel through.

"But why?"

"Why does he do anything?" I reminded

him. "Because he wants to be the one who rules."

"Hmm. There has to be more to it," Geb mused. "Perhaps Thoth will know..."

"No. You can't be thinking of talking to him about us. If anyone finds out about what we've been doing..." The image of the two of us entwined at night sprung to my mind. I pushed it aside. It wasn't that the other gods didn't do the same thing. They did, but most of them took humans to their beds. I wasn't aware of any of the others engaging in the same kind of relationship as we were. Though perhaps they were simply better at hiding it. That wouldn't surprise me.

"Nut..." There was so much emotion in the way he said my name that I softened instantly. "It'll be all right. Even if they do find out, what are they really going to do? It's just threats. They hope we're going to do what they want, because it's easier for them. There's nothing they can actually do to hurt us."

My responding smile was weak but hopeful. Perhaps there was some truth in what he was saying.

"I hope you're right," I whispered.

But inside, I feared he wasn't.

Chapter 5

Despite having arrived perfectly on time, the feast was already in full swing by the time I sat down. All around me, gods and goddesses were drinking, eating, and making merry with one another. I tried not to let the bitterness within me take root. Why was it fine for them to all have the time of their lives, when it wasn't all right for me to spend time with Geb because I enjoyed it and I wanted to? It hardly seemed fair.

But if I wanted to survive amongst the other gods, I had to play by their rules.

My gaze locked with Geb's from where he was sitting across the room. I wasn't sure who was responsible for the seating plan, but this was almost as good as being sat next to him would have been. The two of us would be able to exchange furtive looks, which would make the whole thing more bearable.

"Why do they never tell us the right time for these events?" Taweret asked as she flopped down onto the stool beside me, displeasure written all over her face.

"I'm not sure, I was just thinking the same myself."

"I bet they spend the first couple of hours discussing important matters of state that they don't want our input in," she whispered.

A small snort escaped me. "You're probably right," I agreed.

"One day, it'll be different."

"I'm not sure about that. I doubt Ra will ever give up his power." I nodded towards the sun god, who was lounging on his throne with a smug grin on his face. I couldn't believe some of the others actually put up with him. "Either that, or someone will stage a coup and he'll end up exiled." Now there was something I wished could happen.

"Hopefully, someone who doesn't mind working with the rest of us to make the world a better place." She reached out and snagged a flatbread from one of the passing servers. She tore it in two and offered the other half to me.

"Thanks." I took it from her, marvelling in the warmth it still held. This must have only left the oven a few moments ago.

"This is such a waste of time," she muttered.

"The bread?"

Taweret chuckled. "The feast."

"Oh, that's a given. But so much of what we do seems to be that way. Why is it down to one person alone to do the work of many? Why don't we have help?"

"You're getting more outspoken," she observed.

"Or simply more comfortable expressing my opinions in front of you," I countered. "I'm sorry for being wary of you before."

She shrugged. "That's the way things have to be. It isn't easy to work out who is in alliance with who. For all you knew, I was spying for Ra."

I almost choked on the piece of bread I'd been chewing on. "I doubt that."

"I wouldn't even if he paid me in all the fish he could catch."

I frowned, confused about why she'd chosen fish as her currency until she gestured for another server who came over with a plate full to the brim of cooked fish.

The smell drifted up from the platter, and I waited for it to make my stomach rumble like it normally did. Except that wasn't what happened. Instead, an intense nausea built within me, causing me to gag loudly and pulling Tarewet's attention away from the server.

"What's wrong?"

I tried to respond to her, but retched instead. Taweret waved the server away. I was dimly aware of her sending for some water, and checking around us to see if anyone was paying any attention to us, but I wasn't able to take part in any of it.

"Come on." She latched onto my wrist and tugged me away from the feast, grabbing the pitcher of water the servant offered.

The other goddess ushered me into a

storeroom, hopefully, one that wasn't currently being used.

Given the amount of dust on every available surface, I doubted that was the case.

"What's going on?" she asked me, a serious expression on her normally jovial features.

A cough burst from me as I tried to speak, so she handed me the water. I glugged down several mouthfuls, admittedly feeling a lot better for it.

"I don't know," I admitted to her once I was done.

"Hmm." She looked me up and down, almost as if she was looking for something in particular. I was about to ask her what when she reached out and placed her hands on my stomach.

"Wh..."

"You're pregnant," she announced.

I stared at her, blinking a few times as I tried to process what she'd just said.

"But goddesses don't get pregnant," I countered.

Taweret raised an eyebrow. "Well, you are."

"Oh." What was I going to do? The only

thing I knew for sure was that I needed to tell Geb as soon as possible. We'd gotten into the predicament together, so it stood to reason that he had some say in what we did about it.

"Do you know who the father is?" Taweret asked, bringing my thoughts away from my lover.

I bit my lip and nodded.

She sighed with relief. "That's good. Though I wasn't aware that a human man could make a goddess pregnant," she mused.

"He isn't human," I admitted.

"Oh, well that changes things. No wonder the babies feel so strong."

"Babies?" I echoed.

"Mmhmm, there's more than one of them in there. I'm not sure how many, though, the magic coming from them is too strong and confusing my own."

"That's not good."

She shrugged. "It will all be fine," she promised. "I've done this countless times with humans, it shouldn't be too different for you."

"I need to go tell Geb," I muttered, already heading for the door.

"Ah, I see." She chuckled. "I should have guessed."

"Why would you?" I asked, worrying about what she'd noticed.

"Just a feeling after seeing the two of you together. I think you have something special."

"Please don't tell anyone." It was hard to keep the begging from my voice, but a big part of me didn't care. If the wrong person found out about this, we could be in big trouble.

"Your secret is safe with me," she assured me. "But you'll only be able to keep it quiet for so long. Pregnancies are hard to hide, and I suspect it'll be even more difficult with the power growing inside you."

I nodded. She was right, and I knew it, but hopefully, this could buy us a little bit of time in which to make a plan. At least, that was my hope.

"Thank you," I whispered.

A genuine and affectionate smile spread over her face. "You're welcome. We're friends, and that means we have one another's backs."

"I hope I can repay you for this."

"You don't need to," she countered. "But I

do need you to tell me how Geb reacts, so you should go and find him."

"I will."

She reached out and caught my hand in hers, giving it a reassuring squeeze.

Even though it was such a simple gesture, it truly made me feel like I wasn't alone. I waved at her as I slipped out of the storeroom, determined to find Geb before any more time passed. He needed to know about this. What we had was special already, and the addition of children was only going to make it more so.

Despite the fear thrumming through me, there was also excitement at the prospect of what was to come. I loved him, and the children we were going to have together would only make the bond we shared stronger, I was certain of it.

He wasn't at the seat I'd first spotted him in at this feast. I scanned the room, searching every face in the hope that it would be his. Where could he have gotten to? He'd been spending more time with some of the younger gods recently, but I doubted he'd be off with them at an event as important as this one.

I dismissed a few more clusters of gods, not even bothering to put names to the faces, even though I knew them. I couldn't even have picked out Ra at that moment, even though I was more afraid of him than anyone else in the room.

I turned, knocking into someone's hard chest as I did.

"I'm so sorry," I murmured, pulling away and only then realising it was the one person I'd been looking for.

I let out a sigh of relief.

"Where have you been?" he asked, concern tinting every word.

A lump formed in my throat now it was the time to tell him. I might be excited about it, but I'd never told anyone anything like it before, which meant I had no idea what words I needed to say.

"I was with Taweret..." I started.

Relief crashed over his features. "I lost sight of you, then I couldn't find you again, and I got worried one of the other gods had taken you away."

I frowned. "Why would they have done that?"

He laughed uneasily. "I'm not sure. Just a sense of something being wrong."

"Oh." I paused, using the time to build up the courage I needed. "I'm pregnant, Geb."

A myriad of emotions passed over his face as the news sunk in.

"You...we..." He gulped.

"We're going to have a baby," I confirmed, throwing all caution to the wind. "Well, multiple babies, according to Taweret."

He laughed and swung me up into his arms to dance around. I squealed until he put me down, and the two of us remembered where we were. This wasn't the place to be celebrating our good fortune like this.

"Babies," he whispered.

"What did you say?"

My stomach dropped at the sound of the last person I wanted to hear from right now. Or ever, if I was honest about it.

Slowly, I turned around to find Ra's narrowed eyes boring into me. Everything about him radiated anger.

"You're pregnant?" he asked, his voice surprisingly level.

"Yes." There was no point denying it, he

wouldn't be as angry as this if he hadn't already heard correctly.

"How did this happen?" he demanded.

"The normal way," Geb muttered.

My eyes widened.

"This is unacceptable," Ra continued.

I wanted to point out that it was too late for it to be accepted, it was fact. I was pregnant and that couldn't be undone. At least, I hoped it couldn't.

A sardonic smile twisted at the corners of Ra's lips as he studied the two of us. Fear thrummed through me as a result, and without looking, I slipped my hand into Geb's. If Ra already knew about us, it didn't matter about keeping our feelings for one another a secret.

"You will be cursed," Ra announced calmly. "Nut will not be able to bear any child on any day of the year."

The blood drained from my face. How was that supposed to work? I already had babies inside me, not giving birth to them could cause big problems, not just for me, but for the universe as a whole. It surprised me that he was so willing to risk that in order to curse me.

"You can't do that," Geb insisted, stepping forward to put himself between me and the sun god.

"It's too late. It is done." He turned around and stalked off, leaving the two of us staring after him in disbelief.

Somehow, things had gotten worse than I'd ever expected them to.

Chapter 6

"What are we going to do?" I asked Geb as I paced back and forth in his room. The one small advantage of everything that had happened was that we didn't need to sneak around any more. With Ra already angry at us, and a curse on my head, there wasn't much more anyone could say to make the situation worse.

"We'll think of something," Geb promised.

"Yes, but when? How long is it going to take? Taweret said that human pregnancies last nine months. Is that how long we've got? Or is it going to be different because I'm a goddess?"

"I don't know, Nut."

"Then we need to find out. We can't leave all of this to chance, that's how we're going to end up in even more trouble than we're already in."

"Find out," he echoed, thoughtfulness entering his eyes as he stared at me.

"What? Geb? You're scaring me a little bit."

"I have an idea," he said, reaching out and grabbing my hand before pulling me out of the room and down the corridor.

I stumbled over my own feet before realising the safest thing to do right now was to follow him and see what he was doing. Hopefully, he'd reveal what his plan was before too long.

"Geb? Talk to me?" I begged as we turned down another corridor a little too fast for my liking.

My stomach protested and I had to pull my hand free of his so I could take a moment to chase away the nausea. I hoped this part of the pregnancy would be over soon. Once Geb had finished with whatever his idea was, I should go and find Taweret and ask her what she suggested for making me feel better. I wasn't about to spend the rest of the day almost throwing up.

"Where are we?" I asked after scanning the corridor to try and work it out. Nothing here seemed familiar, but that wasn't too surprising.

"We're here to see Thoth," he told me.

"Oh."

What were we coming to the god of knowledge for? He knew the answers to a lot of things, but I doubted he'd tell us how to remove one of Ra's curses.

We passed through an arch covered in hieroglyphics and stepped into a room with honeycomb-style walls, each filled with several rolls of papyrus. Several human scribes were working at the stone desks situated down the centre of the room. I raised an eyebrow at the sight. If Thoth had already employed several humans to work in his library, then it was only a matter of time before the rest of us had attendants, just like I wanted.

If I managed to survive the next nine

months, then I would bring it up with the other gods and hopefully change the way we all worked for the better. But for now, I had other things to focus on. No one was going to take me seriously while I had Ra's curse hanging over my head.

"Ah, Nut, Geb, I was wondering when you were going to show up," Thoth said, clapping his hands together as he approached us.

"You expected us?" Geb asked.

The other god nodded. "After word spread about your situation at the feast, I thought I'd find you at my door. Why don't you come into the back room and we can talk in peace?"

We followed him past the scribes and out of the library into a second room. While it was smaller than the other one, it appeared to have even more scrolls packed into the walls. Was this simply another storage room, or was it something more private to Thoth? As much as I wanted to know, I kept the question to myself. If he was more likely to help us if we didn't annoy him with overly personal questions.

"What happened?" he asked us.

I exchanged a glance with Geb.

"I thought you knew already?" I asked.

The god nodded. "I'm aware that you are in Ra's displeasure, he made that extremely clear, but no one is aware of the exact nature of what he said to the two of you."

"Oh."

"He's cursed Nut so that she can't give birth," Geb supplied.

Thoth sighed, an even more serious expression than normal gracing his face. "I feared this would happen."

Geb and I exchanged a confused look.

"Feared what exactly?" I asked.

"The day Ra realised he can't hold the throne forever, and that you would bear the child who would usurp him. He's been doing his best to stop the eventuality becoming reality, but has failed spectacularly."

"Oh." I touched my stomach. The swell was still small, but definitely there. Not that I had any doubts about being pregnant. Taweret knew what she was talking about. It was her job as a goddess to understand it and help pregnant women. "But why me?"

"Why do prophecies choose anyone?" Thoth asked. "Perhaps it is simply because you were the first goddess likely to bear children. Or that you were created with an opposite who attracted you. There could be many reasons it was you, or it could be simply a coincidence."

"But Ra's curse causes a problem?" I checked, not so secretly hoping he'd say the curse wouldn't impact us at all and I'd be able to have my children without a problem.

"Unfortunately, yes."

My heart sank in response to Thoth's words. Geb squeezed my hand, reminding me that even if things were dire, I didn't have to go through all of this alone.

"Is there anything we can do?" Geb asked, bringing the conversation back to what we were supposed to be talking about. Ra's motivations might be interesting, but they didn't change anything.

"Preferably without endangering anyone else," I added. The last thing either of us wanted was to make life difficult for any of the others. Ra's wrath was far-reaching and never-ending.

Thoth smiled sadly. "The time has passed for us to avoid asking others for help, but I suspect if you look around, then you will find more people willing than you first suspect."

"That's cryptic," I muttered.

"Or it isn't," he countered. "What were the exact words of Ra's curse?" he asked, taking out a charcoal stick and a sheet of papyrus.

"That Nut should not be able to bear any child upon any day in the year," Geb supplied.

As with the first time I heard the words, horror filled me. How could one god do that to another, even if they were angry? it didn't make any sense to me.

"Ah, specific wording," Thoth mused.

"That's the problem," I pointed out. "He's stopped me from being able to give birth without killing anyone." the moment the words were out of my mouth, I placed my hands on my stomach, as if it would protect the babies inside. I didn't want them exposed to the awfulness of what was happening, even if they were too small and young to understand.

"Ah, dear Nut, you're thinking too literally," Thoth responded with a knowing smile.

"In order to outmanoeuvre him, then we have to find a day that isn't part of the year."

"That isn't possible," I countered, but I wasn't completely convinced. Why would Thoth be mentioning it if it wasn't? He knew almost everything about anything. No one understood how the world worked like he did. I had to trust that he knew what he was talking about.

"We should be able to get Khonsu to move the moon in such a way that we can gain a few extra days," Thoth told us.

"We can't put him in danger too..." I started to protest.

"Don't worry about that. I plan on winning the days from him. No one except the three of us will be blamed," he assured me.

"But I don't want you to be in trouble either," I said quietly.

A grateful expression graced his slender face. "Don't worry about me. Ra needs me too much to turn his anger on me easily. My first duty is to the knowledge of all things in this world, and that includes the babies inside you. I wish to meet them, and to do that, they must be born."

I bit my lip and nodded. As much as I wanted to protest more, I wasn't a fool. He was offering us the help we needed more than anything, and that meant I needed to take it, or my growing family would be doomed before it properly started.

Chapter 7

Geb put his arm around my shoulders and pulled me to him. I leaned against his shoulder, grateful to have his support. Not that there wasn't more of it coming from gods and goddesses all the time. Other than Thoth and Taweret, none of them offered to help us directly, but I kept returning to my rooms and finding gifts for either me or the babies. They wouldn't be doing that if they didn't want to support me.

"We don't have to witness this," he whispered to me.

I sighed loudly. "We do, and you know it. We can't ask either of them to risk themselves for us if we aren't even willing to watch it happen."

He nodded, and the two of us lapsed back into silence as we waited for Thoth and Khonsu to arrive. I wasn't sure how much the moon god had agreed to already, but I doubted he was going to say no if he was already on his way to meet us.

Thoth entered the room first, giving us a tight-lipped smile as he did. That was about as good as it got from the god of wisdom, being stoic was in his nature. I hoped he never changed, there was something very reassuring about his presence and the way he acted. I liked it.

"Good evening, all," Khonsu said brightly as he walked in.

I raised an eyebrow. That wasn't the greeting I'd expected given the circumstances, but I wasn't about to question my good fortune when it was clear a lot could depend on the outcome of this meeting.

"I'm given to understand we're wagering for days outside the normal year?" he asked the three of us.

"Yes," Thoth answered.

"Then I suggest we play senet," Khonsu announced lifting up the arm under which he carried a large board.

He met my gaze and winked, letting understanding dawn on me. Tears sprang to the corners of my eyes as it sunk in that he was doing everything he could to help, without getting himself into trouble. Khonsu was well known for enjoying playing the board game, but he was notoriously bad at it. As far as I knew, he hadn't beaten anyone at it, and if he had, it was only the once.

Had Thoth even managed to plan this?

The god of knowledge avoided looking at me, which suggested he had.

"Very well. You shall play against me," Thoth said. "Best of five?"

"A day for each won game?" Khonsu responded.

"That sounds good to me, why don't you set up?" Thoth gestured to a pair of reed mats already positioned on the floor with two goblets of wine waiting for the gods.

He'd definitely planned this. Or the two of them had together. It didn't matter anyway, for the help they were giving Geb and me, I was going to be eternally in their debts.

I bit my lip as the first game began. It quickly became clear that the rumours about Khonsu's game-playing ability weren't at all exaggerated. It was impressive how badly he was doing when at least part of the success of playing senet was simply down to the luck of the stick toss. Perhaps it was something to do with his magic? It couldn't be anything else.

Even after Thoth had won the second game, I couldn't bring myself to relax. No matter what happened, we had the time we needed for me to give birth. In theory. I didn't imagine it would take longer than a human birth, but maybe I was being foolish to think that. Taweret had been trying to keep a brave face in all the discussions we had about it, but I could tell she was also worried about it. There were too many unknown factors, and it was hard not to solely focus on them.

I bounced my leg up and down as I watched the final few moves of game three. Geb reached out and placed a hand on my knee, giving it a soft squeeze.

"It's all going to be fine," he promised softly.

I sighed. "I hope so, but I can't help but think about all the things that can go wrong. What if Ra finds out about this?" I gestured to the two gods playing senet, though I doubted Geb needed any reminder of what was going on.

"He's not going to," Geb assured me. "No one here is going to tell him. He won't find out about this until it's too late."

"I hope you're right."

"I am. Trust me."

He leaned in and pressed a quick kiss against my cheek. I closed my eyes, enjoying the contact. I truly did hope he was right, even if there was a big part of me that was terrified. The last thing I needed was for Ra to add another curse to me, one was bad enough.

But, now that I thought about it, I knew none of our friends and allies would let that happen. We had more people on our side than before. On the off chance that Ra found out about Thoth and Khonsu's wager, they'd work with us to find another way for me to give birth, I was certain of it. And there was a point where Ra wouldn't be able to curse everyone involved or he'd have a revolt on his hands.

Which meant we needed to spend the next few months making as many friends and connections as possible. Before this whole situation, I wouldn't have thought it was possible, but the past few weeks had shown me how wrong I was about the other deities who lived here. They did care about one another, and it was time I got on board with that. None of them deserved the way I felt about them.

Thoth moved the final game piece of the final match, winning for the fifth time in a row. Even though that meant we'd managed to win five days from the moon god, I still waited nervously for confirmation.

"It seems the three of you have won the days you need," Khonsu said brightly, as if he hadn't just badly lost several games in a row and now owed us a favour.

"Thank you." I met his gaze, hoping he knew what I was really grateful for. It didn't take a genius to work out that he'd suggested doing something he knew he'd lose, and I appreciated the gesture.

"I don't know what you're talking about, Nut. I've just humiliated myself." He winked, confirming my suspicions.

"Then thank you for agreeing to this in the first place."

He shrugged. "I owed Thoth a favour."

"How do we make the days happen?" Geb asked, being far more practical than I was.

"When Nut starts to give birth, come find me. The days won't start until midnight, but I can make them happen from then."

Geb nodded and slumped back in his seat. It wasn't until I saw the relief wash over his face that I realised he hadn't relaxed for the entire time, even if I'd thought otherwise.

"Will it be enough?" I asked quietly, resting a hand on my belly as I did. I hadn't even met the babies inside me and I knew I'd do anything I could to protect them. They were mine, and I wanted them to be safe.

"It should be," Thoth responded. "But if it isn't, we'll figure something out. Now, you should rest and prepare. Everything should be set in place for when we're ready."

The four of us parted ways to go back to our daily duties, and while I was still scared, I had to admit that I felt freer than before.

63

Chapter 8

Pain ripped through me, and I let out a primal scream. What was happening? I'd never felt this way before, it was like my insides were tearing apart and were going to make their way outside my body.

I was dimly aware of the sounds of people scrambling around on the other side of the screen, but even that faded to nothing over the twisting in my abdomen.

"Is everything all right, Nut?" Geb asked as he appeared from the other side of the screen, his face lined with worry.

I grunted out another jolt of pain. "Do I look all right?" I muttered.

He collapsed to his knees and took one of

my hands in his to offer me some comfort. Unfortunately for him, more pain ripped through me and I ended up squeezing his hand to try and cope with it.

To his credit, he winced, but didn't say anything about how much I was hurting him.

"Will you be all right if I go and get Taweret?" he asked.

"Taweret?" I whispered, not under-standing what he meant.

"I think the babies are coming."

"They can't be. We're still within the year..." More of my protest was cut off with another scream.

"I don't think it matters, Nut. They're coming. And if we don't do something about it, then you're going to die."

Panic flooded through me, though I did my best to stop it from taking over me. "We don't know that. This isn't how I'm supposed to be able to die."

"Maybe there's a second way. You know how powerful Ra's curses are."

I nodded, trying not to let fear become the only thing I could focus on.

"I'm going to go find Taweret and send

her to you. I'll come back once I've found Thoth and Khonsu. So long as you can make it to midnight without having the babies, then we should be able to get the five days you need."

Even amidst the pain and distractions, I could appreciate the calm and confident way he sounded.

"Hurry," I whispered.

"I'll be back soon," he promised, leaning in to kiss my forehead. "I love you, Nut."

"Love you too," I gritted out through my teeth. Not because I didn't want him to know, but because the pain was increasing again and it was the only thing I could truly focus on.

Without saying another word, he left. I appreciated that he hadn't asked if I would be all right on my own. The honest answer was that I probably wasn't, but considering the circumstances, it seemed safer not to tell him that or he'd want to stay. Right now, that wasn't an option. We needed the help of our allies or we were never going to manage to safely deliver the babies.

I waited for what felt like an age, but only because of the pain. If I'd been in my normal state, I doubted I'd have even felt that amount of time passing.

Taweret bustled in, heading towards me with a serious expression on her face.

"Oh no," she said the moment she laid eyes on me. "He wasn't wrong."

"Were you hoping he was?"

She chuckled bitterly. "You never know with men, they aren't the best judges when it comes to childbirth."

"They're definitely coming, then?" I asked.

"I'm sorry, Nut, they are."

I closed my eyes, and touched one of my clammy hands to my bulging stomach. I could feel the power pulsing from the babies inside, longing to be out in the world. I wasn't sure how this was going to work. When she'd found out about the situation Geb and I had gotten ourselves into, Taweret had told us that she'd never encountered a pregnant goddess before, and we were going in completely in the dark about the situation. That hadn't been what I wanted to hear at the time, and it was even less of what I wanted to hear now.

"We have to get to midnight," I told her.

She nodded. "I have some amulets and

herbs, but we're mostly going to have to hope that we can buy the others enough time to start the extra days."

The unspoken threat of what could be to come hung between us. At least she wasn't going to try and convince me that everything was automatically going to work out. I wasn't foolish enough to believe that.

Time passed in a haze of pain and torment. I wasn't sure how we were going to get through all of this. I wanted to give up. I needed this to be over. But more than anything, I wanted to see Geb again for the last time.

A thin sheen of sweat covered my entire body, and it was all I could do to keep the babies inside me.

"How long?" I whispered as the stars on my body flared in response to the pain.

"There's an hour left until the day changes," Taweret told me, unable to keep the worry out of her voice.

I reached out for her hand, taking it in mine and giving it a squeeze. "Thank you."

"For what?"

"For being here, and not letting me go

through this alone. I don't suppose they'll be happy with you for doing it."

"If you mean Ra, I don't care what he thinks. Someone needs to teach him a lesson. Perhaps he's right and one of those babies in there will be the one who takes his throne."

I snorted. "Only if they manage to change the days."

"They will."

Shouting sounded from outside my chambers, but when I tried to strain so I could hear it, another scream of pain ripped through me, distracting me completely.

"Nut!" Geb cried.

I was dimly aware of him dropping to the floor beside me. I was too dizzy to be able to make him out properly.

"Is it done?" My voice was hoarser than I expected, but at least I managed to get the words out, even if I was having trouble with them.

"It is. Not long now and we can meet the little one trying to get out."

"There's more than one," I reminded him, sure I'd told him that before.

"How do you know?" he asked.

Now there was a question. "I don't know." I looked at my friend, hoping she'd be able to explain. I'd just taken her word for it.

Taweret chuckled. "Magic," she told us both. "But let's not focus on that for now. We need to get Nut through the next hour still so she can have the babies. I need you to brew me a tisane from the leaves here." She passed something to Geb who nodded and rose to his feet.

After that, it was all about Taweret. She commanded the attention of the room, even if there were only the three of us in it. I was grateful for it. I needed someone who knew what they were doing, and even if she'd never done this for a goddess before, I trusted my friend and knew she'd be able to see us through it.

Chapter 9

I leaned my head back against the wall, exhausted but relieved. The past five days had been a whirlwind of activity, and it hadn't stopped. Each day had brought another child. Three baby gods and two baby goddesses later and I was exhausted. It was a good thing all five of them had already made their way into the world, as our spare time had run out. It turned out we'd needed all of it after all. Something that perhaps Thoth had known the whole time.

"It's over," Geb whispered. "You can relax now." His hand still rested in mine. Despite how horribly I'd shouted at him during the pain, he'd stayed with me the entire time. I'd never loved him more.

I chuckled. "While being the mother to five babies? I doubt I'm ever going to get any rest ever again."

"Except that we're going to live for thousands of years," he countered.

"Unless Ra is particularly vindictive."

"He isn't going to do anything," Taweret assured us as she entered the room with a small bundle in her arms. "It's one thing to punish someone no one knows, but he wouldn't get away with doing the same to you again. Especially not now you have the babies. They're too precious, and everyone knows it." She handed me the bundle and I took it from her.

I pushed the linen away from the tiny face. The baby girl in my arms gurgled and reached out with her tiny hands in a grabbing motion. I was dimly aware of Taweret leaving the room, but I was too focused on the child in front of me. I held out my hand for the baby to play with. She curled her tiny fingers around my dark blue one. I could stare at the contrast between our skin for years and never grow tired of the beauty of it.

A surge of affection rushed through me as I stared down at the perfect little bundle.

"She's already grown," I observed.

"They all have," Taweret agreed as she re-entered carrying our other baby girl. She handed her to Geb who took her gently. "I think they'll grow quickly and be fully grown in a matter of years," she said.

"Oh."

"You sound disappointed."

"I am," I admitted. "I thought I was going to be able to give them the same kind of childhood humans get."

"That might still be possible," my friend reassured me. "There haven't been any child gods up until yours, we have no idea what's going to happen."

I sighed. "And I guess this is my only chance at motherhood too," I observed.

"I don't think Ra is going to let this happen again," Geb agreed. "But how can we stop it? If you get pregnant again, it could kill you."

A shiver ran down my spine.

"I can help there," Taweret promised. "There are amulets and potions you can take. I'll teach you about them later. But for now, I'm going to go and tend to your three boys."

"Do they have names yet?" Geb asked, bringing the second baby closer.

I glanced between the two girls, waiting for the moment where I knew their names. I wasn't sure how I knew that this way would work, but instinct deep within told me it would, especially as I had no idea how I'd gained my name, even though I'd sprung into existence fully grown.

"This one is Isis," I said after a moment, indicating to the baby in my arms. "And the other is Nephthys." Even as the names rolled off my tongue, I knew they were right. I had no idea what these two girls would grow up to do, or even what they'd be goddesses of, but I was certain their names would fit whatever that was.

"Good choices. What about the boys?"

I shook my head. "I won't know for sure until I see them again."

I'd been so busy going through the

motions of birth for five straight days that I hadn't spent much time with any of my children yet. I hoped no human woman would ever have to go through childbirth that long. From the feel of the magic in the room while it had been going on, I figured it was a goddess thing, though I also hoped none of the others would have to go through anything like that. They'd have the advantage of not being cursed to not be able to give birth on any of the days of the year, which certainly hadn't been ideal.

Taweret coughed, drawing our attention to the entrance to my bedchamber.

"Is everything all right?" I asked.

"A messenger from Thoth has just given me this, I thought the two of you would want to see it." She entered the room and handed a scroll of parchment to Geb.

He shifted Nephthys in his arms so he could take it. I waited as patiently as I could for him to read through the hieroglyphics scribbled on it and fill me in, but it was all I could do not to demand he handed it to me as worry started to worm its way through me.

What if Taweret was wrong about Ra not wanting more revenge?

To my surprise, Geb chuckled.

"What is it?" I prompted.

"Thoth said that something went wrong with the way Khonsu called the spare days, and now they need to be part of every year."

"Oh."

"But that he was going to suggest they were used as celebration days to give the humans five days of feasting and time away from their work."

A small smile tugged at the corners of my lips. "So every year, Ra will be reminded that we outsmarted him?" Perhaps I should have been more worried about it, but a big part of me was more amused than anything.

"Yes."

I sighed and leaned back again. Somehow, everything had worked itself out in the end. I would be forever grateful to the people who made that possible. Until the time came that I could return the favour, I would spend my days looking after my children and nurturing the world the best I could. Even if my only domain was the sky and stars, I could make a difference. If I could inspire hope in those who felt like there was no chance of succeeding, then it would be a life well spent.

Epilogue
SEVERAL YEARS LATER

The festival was in full swing, with humans and gods alike doing their best to forget the stresses of the year and have a good time. I watched from a shaded alcove, enjoying the atmosphere, but not wanting to join in directly. Even after years, feasts still filled me with a sense of apprehension, so I tried to participate in them as little as I could. My new priestesses would alert me if anything happened which needed my attention. I was glad I'd finally managed to convince the other gods of the necessity of them. Thoth's help had been invaluable in achieving that.

The clash of metal on metal came from off to the left, drawing my attention to where

Geb was overseeing Osiris and Seth practising with their swords. I smiled at the sight of them, even if it filled me with sadness to see two of my boys growing up so fast. I wasn't sure where the other three had gotten off to, probably to get up to some mischief before they got too old for it. They were all growing at an alarmingly fast rate, and despite the human children born at the same time only being around five years old, my children would reach adulthood in a matter of months. After that, they'd take on their roles as gods. There was already talk among some of the others about making Osiris into some kind of ruler. My eldest boy had all the makings of it, especially as he wasn't as rash as his younger brother.

As if to demonstrate my exact thoughts, Seth made a daring attack with his sword, catching Osiris in the stomach and leaving a thin rivulet of blood. I winced in sympathy, but managed to suppress the urge to run over and help fix the situation. They didn't need me to do that.

"You have your hands full there," Taweret said as she joined me under the shade.

I sighed. "Not for much longer."

"They'll always be your children, Nut. Even when they're thousands of years old, they'll still need their mother."

"I hope so." But I feared it wouldn't be the case. Particularly with Seth, he seemed to detest any form of affection. "Is there any news on their magic?"

She shook her head. "Thoth has determined that their magic and lineage is the same as the rest of ours, though," she said.

"Oh, so we're not their biological parents?" Pain lanced through me at the thought.

"Technically, no. They don't share your blood, or one another's. But that doesn't make them any less yours," she reminded me.

"It's all right, I suspected that was going to be the case." How could it not be? In the years since I'd given birth to the five of them, no other goddess had given birth, or even gotten pregnant, which meant it wasn't anything to do with our own biology and more to do with how the universe wanted to bring about more gods and goddesses.

"It's better for them," Taweret assured me.

"They'll stand out because of what they accomplish, rather than how they were conceived."

"You're right, that is much better," I agreed, and could potentially be used in order to keep Ra off their backs.

Cheers sounded from one of the wrestling matches happening a few streets over. Someone must have won a match if the response was anything to go by. I was grateful to be here with some of my family and one of my friends instead of watching two men fight for a non-existent prize.

"Did you hear a new goddess came into being recently?" Taweret asked.

"Oh?" It was a fairly regular event now, with more and more of our kind popping up as the years went on. I suspected it was because the humans were growing more numerous, and once enough of them believed in a certain deity, they came into being. Or something like that. I wasn't sure of the specifics.

"I can't remember her name, she's a goddess of dance."

"Dance?" I echoed. That was an interesting one, though I could understand why she had come about, dancers were now at every event providing entertainment.

"Mmhmm. Apparently, Amun was very taken with her."

I raised an eyebrow. "How unusual."

"I know. I almost thought he wasn't interested in anyone at all."

"Nothing will come of it," I told her.

She shrugged. "Perhaps not, but it'll be interesting to see. A lot more of the gods and goddesses have started romantic relationships since everything you and Geb went through."

"I'm glad. The more good comes from it, the more worth it the situation was."

She reached out and placed a hand on my shoulder. "A lot of good has come from it already," she assured me.

"I know."

She wasn't wrong. I'd found good friends, gained a family, and finally managed to change the lives of the people I lived around for the better. It was all I'd ever wanted to do and more. I couldn't wait to see what the future would bring and how much more I could make better by being a part of it.

Thank you for reading *Mistress Of Sky And Stars*, I hope you enjoyed it! If you want to see what happens when the court of gods is more established, you can in the main *Forgotten Gods* series, starting with *Feather Of Balance*: https://books.authorlauragreenwood.co.uk/featherofbalance

And if you want to try your hand at playing senet (and find out if you would have what it takes to beat Khonsu!) you can download a board and instructions for free here: https://books.authorlauragreenwood.co.uk/senet-fg

Author Note

Thank you for reading Mistress Of Sky And Stars, I hope you enjoyed Nut and Geb's story. This wasn't one I planned on writing when I first started working on the Forgotten Gods books, but once I reopened the main series, I knew I had to. There was something about the story that begged to be written about, perhaps it was because they succeed against all of the odds.

The elements of this story are reasonably close to those of the original myth. One of the main changes is that Taweret wasn't mentioned in the original, but it felt wrong to have Nut go through her pregnancy without a friend or any help from another woman, which was why Taweret (a real goddess of fertility heavily linked to pregnancy and childbirth) found her place in the story. In reality, Taweret didn't become popular until the Ancient Egyptian New Kingdom, though as that is when most creation stories (such as the one that this story is based on) rose to prominence, I thought this was a fair addition. Aspects of Taweret and other hippo-headed protection goddesses are recorded as far back as the Old Kingdom. The other difference is that of Tefnut and Shu. As the Ancient Egyptian gods were more about their aspects than personalities (in contrast to their Greek counterparts), they weren't considered as standoffish in the original myth - though in the original, Shu is ordered to stand between Nut and Geb to stop them having sex (which is a little strange when he is also supposed to be their Father).

If you noticed that the name of Nut and Geb's fifth child was omitted, then this was on purpose. In some stories, they only have four children over the five days instead of five, but it depends on which version of the myth is being cited. The fifth child is called Horus the

Elder (not to be confused with Horus the son of Isis and Osiris). That confusion is why I didn't name him in the book itself, I wanted to make things as easy for everyone as possible. I could have omitted his existence completely, but the five children, one on each day, is so much neater than the alternative.

Many of the family ties between the gods have been removed in my Forgotten Gods Universe, this is because of a couple of reasons, the main one being that it means there is less chance of incest, which isn't particularly romantic. The other reason for this is because the family ties meant different things to the Ancient Egyptians when it was about the gods. For example, Nut, Geb, Tefnut, and Shu are considered a family because they all represent aspects that are closely linked together (the sky, earth, moisture, and air respectively), while Nut and Geb are consorts because their aspects are seen as opposites. To the Ancient Egyptians, it was more about how things fit together than who shared blood with who. This is also helped by there being multiple versions of how each god or goddess came into being (especially for major gods like these) some of which contradict one another.

Some of the characters mentioned in the story have their own books within the Forgotten Gods Universe. You'll find Isis and Osiris' story in *Queen Of The Two Lands*, Nephthys' in *Empress Of The Dark*, and Amun and Hathor (the dance goddess) are the romantic leads in *Quest Of the Goddess* (while Khonsu also plays an important role in their story). Thoth can be found in *Collector Of Sand And Tears*. Taweret also has a story of her own in *Bringer Of The River Waters*. That was never part of my plan either, but by getting to know her alongside Nut, I started to gain an insight into what a story from her would look like.

You can join my Facebook Reader Group or Mailing List for updates when I have news!

Stay safe and happy reading!

- Laura

Get A Free Forgotten Gods Story

A hippo goddess and a crocodile god are needed to help the Nile before it's too late.

When the river Nile doesn't flood like it's supposed to, the gods turn to hippo goddess, Taweret, to help with the problem.

Even with Taweret and Sobek's collective magic, they fail to find the problem, until they come across Isis on the side of the Nile.

Can they bring back the floods before it's too late?

-

Bringer Of The River Waters is an origin story to the Forgotten Gods series and is based on Egyptian mythology. It includes a dash of adventure, a m/f romance, and can be read as a standalone.

If you enjoy Egyptian mythology, gods and goddesses, quests and adventures, and a modern setting, then you should start the Forgotten Gods series!

You can download Mistress Of Sky And Stars for free here: https://books. authorlauragreenwood.co.uk/taweretfg

Also by Laura Greenwood

You can find out more about each of my series on my website.

- Obscure Academy: a paranormal romance series set at a university-age academy for mixed supernaturals. Each book follows a different couple.
- The Apprentice Of Anubis: an urban fantasy series set in an alternative world where the Ancient Egyptian Empire never fell. It follows a new apprentice to the temple of Anubis as she learns about her new role.
- Forgotten Gods: a paranormal adventure romance series inspired by Egyptian mythology. Each book follows a different Ancient Egyptian goddess.
- Amethyst's Wand Shop Mysteries (with Arizona Tape): an urban fantasy murder mystery series following a witch who teams up with a detective to solve murders. Each book includes a different murder.
- Grimm Academy: a fantasy fairy tale

academy series. Each book follows a different fairy tale heroine.

- Jinx Paranormal Dating Agency: a paranormal romance series based on worldwide mythology where paranormals and deities take part in events organised by the Jinx Dating Agency. Each book follows a different couple.
- Purple Oak Oasis (with Arizona Tape): a cozy fantasy romance series with unusual magic. Each book follows a different couple.
- House Of Blood And Roses: a vampire romantasy series following a heroine who discovers she's a vampire noble and has to navigate a world full of politics, betrayal, and blood lust.
- Scales Of Justice: an urban fantasy following a thief who accidentally becomes the newest apprentice of the goddess of truth.
- Speed Dating With The Denizens Of The Underworld (shared world): a paranormal romance shared world based on mythology from around the world. Each book follows a different couple.
- Blackthorn Academy For Supernaturals (shared world): a

paranormal monster romance shared world based at Blackthorn Academy. Each book follows a different couple.

You can find a complete list of all my books on my website:

https://books.authorlauragreenwood.co.uk/book-list

Signed Paperback & Merchandise:

You can find signed paperbacks, hardcovers, and merchandise based on my series (including stickers, magnets, face masks, and more!) via my website:

https://books.authorlauragreenwood.co.uk/shop

About Laura Greenwood

Laura is a USA Today Bestselling Author of paranormal romance, urban fantasy, and fantasy romance. When she's not writing, she drinks a lot of tea, tries to resist French macarons, and works towards a diploma in Egyptology. She lives in the UK, where most of her books are set. Laura specialises in quick reads, with healthy relationships and consent-positive moments regardless of if she's writing light-hearted romance, mythology-heavy urban fantasy, or anything in between.

Follow Laura Greenwood

- Website: www.authorlaura-greenwood.co.uk
- Mailing List: https://books.authorlauragreenwood.co.uk/newsletter
- Facebook Group: http://facebook.